Meet the Minions

Simon and Schuster
First published in Great Britain in 2014 by Simon and Schuster UK Ltd
1st Floor, 222 Gray's Inn Road, London, WC1X 8HB
A CBS Company

Originally published in 2013 in USA by Little Brown and Company

ISBN 978-1-4711-2368-9
2 4 6 8 10 9 7 5 3 1

Printed and bound in China
www.simonandschuster.co.uk
www.despicable.me

Meet the Minions

Adapted by Lucy Rosen
Based on the Motion Picture Screenplay
Written by Cinco Paul & Ken Daurio

SIMON AND SCHUSTER
London   New York   Sydney   Toronto   New Delhi

Hi, *Despicable Me 2* fans! Can you spot these items in this book?

Minion

Dragon Kyle

Fruit

Jar

Meet Dave and Kevin and Tom
and Stuart and Jerry.
They are all Minions.

They are just a few
of the army of Minions who work
in Gru's secret underground lab!

The Minions have one job,
and one job only:
they work for Gru.

The Minions love to
carry out his master plans.
Sometimes, they do not watch out
and can make a mess.

Once upon a time,
Gru was a super villain!
He even stole the moon
with the help of the Minions!

That was before Gru became a dad
to three girls.
Now, the Minions help him
raise Margo, Agnes and Edith!
It can be just as hard!

The Minions help
with more than the girls.
They also help Gru
with his new business.

$$\frac{2yx}{g7\sim} \times \frac{a3^2bc\,99}{\infty\,phmn5}$$

$$profit = \frac{8° \times n - 1}{(berries)}$$

"My life of crime is over," says Gru.
"Now I am doing something sweeter.
Behold, my recipe for jams and jellies!"

Dave puts up a sign that says
"Testing in Progress".
Some Minions start to mash fruit.
Others just make a mess.

At last, a jar is complete.
Gru calls the jam
Mr. Gru's Old-Fashioned Jelly!
The Minions cheer—
until they taste it.
Yuck!

It may not be as exciting
as stealing the moon,
but Gru, the Minions and the girls
seem pretty happy anyway.

When it is Agnes's birthday,
Gru throws her a princess party.
He invites her friends,
and they come in fun costumes.

"A dragon is coming!" says Agnes.
Kyle, their pet, is dressed up
as a dragon.

"Call the knights!" says Margo.
The Minions march out
wearing tiny suits of armour.
The Minions are the knights!

They pretend to attack Dragon Kyle.
They end up fighting one another.
Agnes laughs and tells them,
"Fight the dragon, not one another!"

The next day,
something strange happens.
A mysterious car appears
on the street.

Gru leaves the house
to check it out.
In a fiery flash, he is gone!
Someone has taken him!

Tom and Stuart
peek around the corner
just in time to see Gru disappear.
"Boss! Boss!" they shout
as the car drives away.

Tom and Stuart look at each other.
They know they have to act fast.
Gru is in trouble,
and the Minions have to help.

Tom leaps and lands on the car!
Stuart tries to jump too,
but his dungarees get stuck.
He is pulled along.

The woman driving the car
is a secret agent named Lucy.
She spots the Minions
and captures them, too!
She zaps them with an AVL-Issued
Lipstick!

Lucy takes Gru and the Minions
to the headquarters of
the Anti-Villain League.
"Gru, we need your help," says Lucy,
"to save the world from a super villain."

Gru thinks about the job offer.
He knows his jelly tastes gross,
so he and the Minions say yes!
It will be more fun to be super spies!

Back at home,
Gru, Tom and Stuart
tell the other Minions
about their new mission.
All the Minions cheer!

The Minions never liked
the yucky jelly anyway.
They happily smash all the jelly jars.

Gru is happier than ever.
He has a loving family,
an awesome new job
and many Minions!